Silent Night

Tony Bower

malcolm down

PUBLISHING

A special word of thanks to Lydia for her skilful editing, encouragement and wonderful support.

A big thank you to Claire for her beautiful artwork on the cover.

This book is dedicated to my son, Joseph.

'Greater love has no one than this:
to lay down one's life for one's friends'

(John 15:13)

Introduction

In the midst of madness, a peace beyond measure
In the midst of chaos, a calm
In the midst of a horrific war, a hope
in wounded hearts

The Christmas Truce of 1914 is a story that stirs the soul. Much has been written about this singular event that appears like the eye of a hurricane, granting a moment's peace in the harshest of battlefields.

This free verse story is a fictional account of one man's struggle in the insanity of the trenches.

This story is set with the backdrop of that amazing Christmas Truce.

No more details and no spoilers! I hope that this story can convey a glimpse into a war beyond the scope of our imagination. I also hope that this story shows that even in the worst of wars, there is still a hope and a peace because of the Christ child of Christmas.

Tony Bower

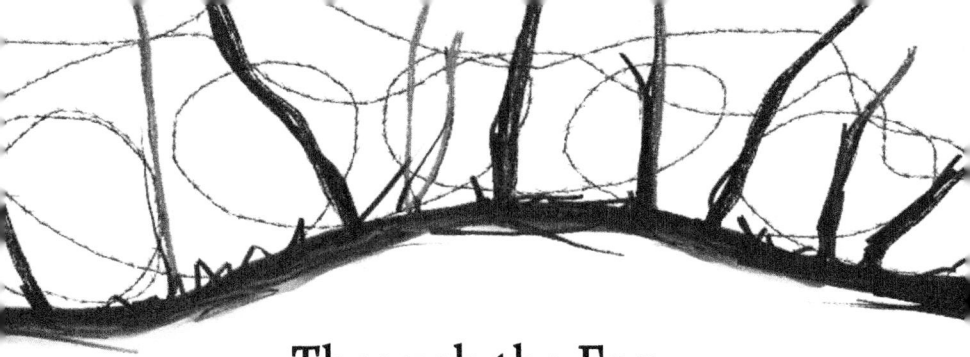

Through the Fog

They are coming
Through the fog
Through the mists
They are coming

I need to defend myself
I need to be ready to fire

But I can't

    I can't

My fingers are too cold
Too numb
The trigger is too tight

They are coming
Through the fog
Through the mists
They are coming

    The sun is shining
    It is brighter than gold
    It is warm on my face
    It is a gift of grace

I am down by the river
It is summer
And Ellie is laughing
I am trying to swing
Over the water
When the rope breaks
And SPLASH!

    I fall into the river
    I plunge into the cold water
    Gasping
    For breath
    Reaching out
    For a hand
    To take hold
    Like a lifeline
    Like a lasting lifeline

Ellie is crying now
    and
It isn't water on my body

But gas
Lethal, deadly gas
And Ellie is crying

They are coming
Through the fog
Through the mists
The Germans
Are coming

4

And the rifle
In my hand
Is as heavy as lead
And as dead
As a dodo
And the Germans
The Germans
Are coming

We Are All Screaming

'Wake up!'

   'WAKE
   UP!'

The words cut through
Like barbed wire
And I am here
Back in the land of the living
If you can call it that

'You were having a nightmare'
   A voice as light as snow says

I don't recognise the man
He's young
   So young

We all are
   So young

He has a ginger moustache
And a friendly smile

'Ben'

He says

'My name is Ben'
   He tells me

'I am sorry'

'I am sorry to . . . disturb you'
   He says as he watches my face like a parent caring
for a sick child

Ben smiles warmly as he tells me
'We all scream.
Not everyone screams out loud'
He adds
with an elephant weight of experience in his words
'But we are all screaming'
There is a kindness in his voice
An understanding

'What's your name, soldier?'

'Harry,' I tell him
'My name is Harry'

Ben holds out his hand
And I take it
And shake it warmly
   And I take it
   Wondering if
   This is a lifeline
   Or just another passing shifting shadow
   And another waste of life
   In this cruelest of times

Horrible Choking Smoke

'Good morning Harry,' he says

    Although the word
    'Good'
    Does not make any sense
    Not in my nightmare
    Waking or asleep

    This
    Is
    A
    Nightmare

    A living

    Hell

    A battlefield of darkness

    A field of broken dreams

    A graveyard of all hopes

'It's good to meet you'

    He continues to speak
    Though I am not really listening
    His words like wisps of cloud

Of gun fire smoke
Drifting

Drifting

Drifting over my head

'I'm the new chaplain
And as it is almost Christmas
I have come bearing gifts'

And with that
He reaches inside his top pocket

And I know he is not a magician
I know there is no rabbit
He is going to pull out of his captain's hat
No magic wand
That can be waved
To make this evil war
Suddenly disappear

And

V

A

N

I

S

H

Back into its own horrible choking smoke

I Shot a Man

It's a gospel
  Not a rabbit
  Nor a wand

A small pocketbook gospel

John's gospel

I look at Ben trying to conceal
  My surprise
  My lack of faith
  In any words that can make
  Any kind of difference

  I try to not reveal
  My indifference
  My insolence
  To a book my family
  Revere

'Thanks'
I tell him
  With no feeling or meaning

'But no thanks'
  I say with true conviction
  My words puncturing his smile
  Puncturing his hope

Ben looks back
Doesn't say anything
He's waiting
And I'm tired
So tired
Tired of the killing
Tired of . . .
Tired of living
If this is what you call
Living

Ben waits
Makes himself comfortable
Doesn't say a word
Just sits down
On an old wooden box

A distant boom breaks the silence

'You didn't even flinch' Ben says

I look at him
Stare into his eyes
Allow him to see into my soul
So that he knows why
Why I don't want to read the book
Why I lost mine in the battle
Why I can hardly speak
Why I can hardly live

But don't want to die

I'm seventeen years old
And a few hours ago
I shot a man

A few hours ago

I pulled my trigger

Heard my gun

FIRE!

Like the fire of Hell

I held the trigger tight
Held it firm with all my trembling might

I
Shot
A
Man

And felt the darkness hold me
And engulf me
And whisper

'You will never see the light
Ever, ever, ever'

I
Shot
A
Man

I
Shot
A
Man

And my world is over
And my life

And this war will never be
Over

What Mercy?

I shot a man
And watched him fall
And then I walked over to him
Laying there on the ground
Remembering how many
How many of my mates
Are no longer here
So that when I got to him
My bayonet was raised
And he wasn't going anywhere
He was laying with his face
Half in the mud
Half staring into no man's land
One lone wolf
Facing another
From a different tribe
The best shot at the country summer fair
The crack sniper, the army said
When they saw me shoot
When they first told me
I felt proud
Pride in my country
And pride in myself
But there is nothing to feel proud about

When you're aiming not at a coconut shy
But a man's skull
So I stood there
Watching him
Like an animal
Over its prey
And I stood there
Waiting to avenge

All those who had fallen
All those who wouldn't be playing
Their football in England again

My mates

My team

Dead
And gone

And here was the enemy
For the first time
With a face I could see
Wounded by me
And at my mercy

At my mercy

At

   My

   Mercy

   What mercy?

   What

   Mercy?

A Boy Like Me

I stood there
Bayonet raised
Above my head
Until my arms began to ache

I stood there
With my weapon raised
Until I knew

I couldn't kill this man

Not like this

No matter what I'd seen
And no matter
How many of my friends
I'd lost

I couldn't take this life
It wasn't right
None of this is right
None of it

I looked into the man's eyes
I say man
But he was a boy
A boy like me

A boy caught up
In Hell
   And so
I turned away
Not able to help him
Not sure if I'd saved him
Or killed him

Too numb
Too lost
In my own world
   To know what I was thinking
   Or what I was feeling

   What feeling?

I turned my back

   Turned my back
   On the lone wolf

   Turned my back
   On the wounded wolf

   Turned my back
   On the dying wolf

And trudged back through the sludge

Trudged back through the sludge
   Trudged back
   Trudged back through the wastelands

The wastelands
Of a thousand wasted souls

Trudged with my rifle
Hanging limp

Trudged with my heart
Slumped
Slumped beyond hope
Slumped to a place so dark
I had forgotten what light was
And so, as this man
With a friendly smile
Offers me a book
And a story, I say 'No'

I say

   'No'

I don't look him in the eyes

I don't look into his face

I don't ask for his understanding
Or his sympathy
Or empathy

I don't ask him to help me
Pray for me
Or ask if God can ever forgive me

And so, I say

   'No'

A Fable or Fantasy?

It was Bill who began it
Bill
The stretcher bearer
Bill
Singing in a deep voice
Bill
Cutting through the silence
Of a tombstone trench

'God rest ye merry gentlemen
Let nothing ye dismay
For Jesus Christ your Saviour
Was born on Christmas Day
To save the world
From Satan's power
When we had gone astray
O tidings of comfort and joy
Comfort and joy
O tidings of comfort and joy'

Ben looks at me
And smiles

I feel no comfort
Know no joy

But I know
We need saving
From this hellish land
What I don't know
Is that there is a Saviour

'Are you sure you don't want that book?'
Ben asks

  The question hangs like a Christmas decoration
  waiting for the festivities to begin

Bill is still singing
His voice hauntingly floating through the air

  The words ringing like bells

  Ringing bells in my mind

  Reminding me of times as a child
  Times when I loved Christmas
  And loved being in church at Christmas

  The words are sounding bells
  In my memory
  Like a faint flicker
  Of a dying fire
  Embers of memories
  Trying to spark back
  Into life

I am no longer sure
What I believe in
But in my world of darkness
That carol

Has lit a tiny spark of something

I hesitate

And Ben patiently waits

He looks at me
As if he is reading me like a book

'It's a great story,' he says

'But it's not a fable story
Or a piece of history
It's our story, it's THE story'

A fable?

A fantasy?

A piece of history?

A story?

THE story?

A fable or a miracle child
Born in a stable?

A fantasy or a miracle of a risen
Saviour?

This story

His Story

Wandering

There is the flutter of snowflakes
Drifting down
Softly down
Pure white
Landing
In the deepest mud imaginable
It's almost Christmas
And it's snowing

Ben looks up at the sky
And smiles

'I love snow'
He says

'I used to'
I reply

'Pure crystals from Heaven'
He says

I look down at where they land
In the grime and the filth

'Not pure anymore are they?'
I tell him

'Not once they touch this scarred earth'
   I say
   Looking at the pure white
   Turning into filthy mush

Ben waits

He does that

He looks at me
But I can't tell what he's thinking

'Harry, please let me tell you a story'

   He looks at me
   And I don't look away

   But as he looks at me
   I don't know what to say
   As Ben continues to talk
   And as he starts to say . . .

'It's a story about pure love
Coming down from Heaven
   Someone sacred
   Someone like no one else
   Who has ever lived on earth
   because this was Heaven's child
   touching earth'

   Ben pauses
   And looks like he's about to pray
   Before he carries on speaking
   And his words powerfully saying

'Jesus touching what was scarred
And taking upon Himself the scars of humanity'

I look at him
As the snow thickens
And the cold begins to bite
Through the threads of my uniform

'Sounds like you've just told me the story'
I say with a wry grin

Ben smiles
'It's what changed my life
From being an angry young man
With wealth and position
Wasting it all away, until . . . well until that day'

Ben stops talking
  And it looks like his mind
  Has gone

  W
  A
  N
  D
  E
  R
  I
  N
  G

  Wandering down a murky past
  Wandering down a dark dead-end alley

  Ben suddenly snaps back into the moment
  Into the present
  And as he looks at me
  He continues to tell me his story

Shouts Through the Silence

'I come from a privileged background
Money was not in short supply
All that I wanted
I got
But I found that the more I took
The less I had
In here'

Ben pauses
And points to his chest

'I made a good friend at university
He was a great cricketer
And someone I admired

He was also a Christian
Who knew and loved God
And also knew that God
Loved him'

Ben pauses
There was more to his story
More to be said
But I wasn't going to hear it

Not then I wasn't

Not when there were shouts

All around me
And the sound of machine gunfire
Breaking through
The silence of the snowflakes

'Someone's caught on the wire!'
I hear a soldier say
And before I could even blink
Ben is on his feet
And moving fast

He looks like a centre forward

Chasing after a through ball
Chasing in on a gaping goal

He looks like a sprinter
In an Olympic final
He looks like a sprinter
Sprinting for a gold medal

He looks like a man
Racing to his destiny
He looks like a man
Rushing towards eternity

An eternity of what?

Heaven
Or
Hell?

Hell
Or
Heaven?

Is anything waiting for Ben
As he rushed out into the bleakest
And darkest of nights

Out into Darkness

The snow is falling thicker than ever
The stars as cold as ice
As I look up into a peaceful sky
No sight of angels tonight
But sounds of demon guns
And the screams of tortured lives

Ben has gone
Out of the trench
And out of my sight

I feel numb
Not just with fatigue
But with the endless slaughter

I sit still
Hardly able to move
Watching the silent stars
Watching me
If there is a God in Heaven
We need him on earth
Right now
Then it hit me
Ben
He was out there right now

Probably risking his life
And for what?
And for who?
I gulp in the frosty air
Brush the snowflakes
From my uniform
And reach for my rifle
'Heaven help me'
I mutter
'Heaven help me'
    I say
    As I stumble out into the dark

    'Heaven help me?'
    I ask as a question
    As I begin to make a move

    'Heaven help me'
    I plead as I head
    Out
    Of my trench

    And as I head out
    Into
    The walls of darkness

One Way Ticket
to the Graveyard

'It's Eric'

The words hung in the dark sky
Frozen in the wind

'He's caught on the wire'

There are people moving
Quietly now
A sense of dread and fear settling
Faster than the falling snow

No man's land
Dead bones
And snipers' bullets
Deadly gas
And a myriad of ways to suffer
Before your life is taken

No man's land
Where no man should ever be
But the place
And the space where Eric is

Caught in a web of cruel wire
Cutting through skin and bone

'What's happening?' I ask
Feeling a chill run through me
A chill that has nothing to do with icy winds
Or the snows of winter
'Captain Hamilton is going over the top'
    Someone replies

The name rings no bells
And for a moment I am clueless
Before my mind races to the answer

'Ben!'

Jack, our rifleman, stares at me

'You know him?' he asks

'I . . . no . . . well . . . I just met him'

Jack nods
'Brave soul' says Jack
'And a vicar too, as well as a captain'

'But if he's going over the top?'

Jack lights a cigarette
And blows out the smoke

'Then he's on a . . .'
Jack offers me a cigarette
'One way ticket to the graveyard'
He mutters
As his cigarette lights up a falling snowflake

And as I watch the snowflake flutter and fall
    In this never-ending darkness

And as I watch the snowflake descend in the
darkness
I think about Ben disappearing into a greater
darkness

Standing in the trench
Standing and straining to see
This brave heart that has just taken his one
way ticket

To the graveyard

Into No Man's Land

There is a silence
An eerie silence
Like the world is holding its breath
Watching
And waiting
Like the axe
About to fall
Like the finger poised
On the trigger
There is a moment
Of deadly quiet
But all is far from calm

Jack puts his hand on my shoulder
Spooking me out

'Don't do that Jack!'
Jack laughs
And flicks some ash from his fingers

'You look like you've seen a ghost,' he says
Taking a deep drag of his cigarette

'Did you try and stop Ben?' I ask him

Jack's eyes lock onto mine

Dark and soulful as he replies
'If he wants his own funeral
That's his choice
That just means there's less bodies
To bury'

Maybe it was the heartlessness
In his voice

Maybe it was something else stirring within
But for whatever reason
Or whatever madness
I find myself moving towards the ladder

'Ere, what you doing?'
   A voice calls out

I place one hand on the ladder
And gaze back at a cigarette-silhouetted Jack

'Don't worry, Jack
There'll be more smokes for you'

All I hear is Jack coughing
As I climb out of the trench

   Jack's voice fades into the night
   As I crouch down low
   And begin to crawl
   And begin to go

   Into

   No

   Man's

   Land

A Bullet Flying
with Icy Death

There is darkness
A sea of darkness
A no man's land
Of memories
Memories
I have to push back
Push away

Memories
Like the gas
That would choke me

Memories
Like my friends
That I have had to bury

'Captain?'

Silence

'Captain?'

Snow swirling
In the black night

'Ben?'

More white silence

'BEN!'

I lower my body to the ground
Out of instinct
When you raise your voice
Make an audible sound
In the middle of Hell
You are bound to find a demon somewhere

'BANG!'

The gunfire sounds loud
In the winter snow
A bullet somewhere flying
With icy death

I lie low
Breathing hard

Ben, where are you?
Why are you here?
Why am I here?

More gunfire
More bullets
More shouts
Only this time I hear a voice
One I recognise
It is a man crying out
And I know to the chill of my soul
It is Ben

As the Stars Watch On

For a moment
I don't move
Don't even breathe
The gunfire ceases
The cries drift away like falling snow

For a moment
There is a surreal peace
In the midst of this madness
And my mind remembers playing games
Of hide and seek when I was a boy
But I know with painful dread
That this is no childish game
But a hellish battlefield
Where there are no winners
Just fallen soldiers

Is Ben one of them?
Do I crawl back to my trench?
Do I try to save my own skin?

I bury my head
Then gaze up at a sky of silent stars
'Oh God, oh God
If there be a Heaven above

If there be a hope for mankind
Let there be a sign on earth
Right now'

I wait
In the quiet
I wait
And all I can hear
Is the sound
Of my shallow breath
The sound of my shallow breath

    In the deathly quiet
    In this hell on earth
    As I gaze up to the heavens
    And ask

    If there is a God listening?

    If there is a God caring?

    For this hell
    On earth

'No one wants to die at Christmas'
I mutter

As I begin to crawl
Not back towards our trench
But forwards
Towards the wire
Towards the waiting guns
As the stars watch on
In grave silence
And the universe
Holds its breath

Drifting Away

I see a man silhouetted
Still
Like a statue
But grotesque
Like a puppet
Without strings
Dangling limply
Another victim
Of a barbaric battle
And in the cold
Of winter's deep night
I want to go to sleep
Close my eyes
And drift away
Like falling snow
In the night I want to
Let go
Of everything
I do it
I close my eyes
Let them shut tight
Shut out a world gone wild
Shut out the suffering
Shut out the shots that ring constantly

Through tortured day
And tormented night
I close my eyes
And rest my head
The snow is quite thick now
Icy
But comforting
It becomes my white pillow

The flakes landing on my body
A clean blanket
Soon I will be covered from head to toe
My face is numb
There is tingling
Running through my fingers
But I don't want to move
I don't want to be part of this world anymore
I just want to sleep
My eyes are tight shut
The snow is gently falling
And I am drifting away

'HARRY!'

Anywhere at All

I'm dreaming
The voice is from a distant place
A forgotten time
A memory

'HARRY!'

Although it does sound real

'HARRY!'

Very real
   As
My eyes flicker open
   And
I am suddenly wide awake

There is a voice calling
Someone who knows me
Who has seen me
Who is aware I am here
Someone who is still alive

I brush away the snow from my eyes
And stare hard at the wire

The figure hasn't moved

I am sure of that as
I peer into the darkness
Hoping for the clouds to move
For the moon to shine bright
Not making me a target
But revealing who is out there

'HARRY!'

'Yeah'
My voice cracks
From the cold
From the fear
From the lack of feeling

'It's Ben'

    'Where are you?'

    I should have guessed
    I should have known
    And I should have seen him too

    He isn't far away
    Not when I look in the right direction
    He isn't far away at all
    But from the look of him
    And the way his body is twisted
    And sprawled in the snow
    It doesn't look like
    He will be going anywhere
    At all

'Why did you come?'

'You've been shot!'
   I exclaim

'You came'
   Ben says through gritted teeth

'Can you move?'
   I ask

'Why did you come?'
   He answers

'For a nice cup of tea
Why do you think?'

'Thank you'
   He says

Ben tries to sit up
But falls back

'Can you move?'
   I ask him

'Not really'
   He tells me

I look around me
Try to work out the distance I have travelled

Try to think through my steps
And how possible it would be
To carry Ben back to the trench

'You can save yourself'
Says Ben
And his voice tells me
He means it

I look down at him
And reply
'But you didn't
    You didn't try to save yourself
    You tried to save someone'

Ben says nothing
As I look around

The snow's almost stopped now
Making us more of a target

'This might hurt'
I tell Ben

'I think there is no might about it'
Grimaces Ben
As I hoist him onto my back
Ignoring the wincing he makes
And ignoring the weight he is
And ignoring the danger
I am putting us both in

The truth is
Ben would die if I did nothing
And by doing something
I might just be about
To get us both killed

'You don't have to do this, Harry
You can save yourself'

I ignore Ben
As I stand up
And make us both
   A big
   Big

   TARGET

An Unexpected Way

When you have no strength
But somehow you find some
When you can't go on
But somehow you do
When you can't see where you are going
But somehow you find your way
When you stumble every step
But somehow don't fall
When you think you are lost
But somehow you win through
That's how it was
Beyond any explanation
Or rational reason
There wasn't one shot that rang out
One voice raised in anger
Not one moment when our lives
Were suddenly threatened
As I staggered back to our trench
Even the moon was beaming
As I slumped over the line
And fell in a heap

'Ere look, it's Harry!'

There are cheers going up
Loud cheers
And people running
I can hear them running
Feel hands on my back
And people clapping
I am alive
I am alive!
It was a miracle
If you believe in miracles

Do I believe in miracles?
    I don't know
    But I do know
A man who does

'Ben?'
I look down

'Captain?'

'Captain!'

He's not moving
He's not moving
Just a dead weight on the floor
And he's not

Moving

He's Not Smiling

It takes Bill to make anything happen
I can't move
And Jack is too busy lighting a cigarette
To lift a finger to help anyone

Bill moves
Fast
He's bending down
Checking for breathing
Speaking softly
And checking
All the time checking

He can't be dead
He can't
Can he?
After all of this
After everything that's happened
He can't be dead
He can't

'Is he . . .'
I can't say the word
If I say the word
It will be true

It will be real
It will make it final
If I say the word

I can't
I won't say it
And it won't be real
Bill lifts his face
He's not smiling
Why is he not smiling?

    Why have they stopped cheering?
    Why is Jack just stood there smoking?

    'Tell me, Bill
    Please tell me
    Tell me he's alive'

    Bill looks up at the sky
    Why?
    Then he kneels beside me
    And puts his hand
    On my shoulder
    And he tells me
    Bill tells me

More Human

'He's alive'
The words are whispers
They are also a lifeline
He's alive
He's alive!
Ben made it
We made it
'But . . .'
And the word hangs
Like an executioner's axe
Like a rope around the neck
The word hangs
As we carry him to quarters
Settle him down
Get blankets
A hot drink
Put on bandages
And bind up his wound
There is blood
Oozing
We try to stem the flow
Try to keep his pale snow-like face
From breathing its last
The medic comes

And tries not to give the last rites
As I pace the tiny room
And find myself praying
No one can hear me
My words are whispers
No man can hear me
But does God?

Does God hear?
Is He there?
And does He care?

I look at Ben
A man I barely know
But a man who risked his life
    To save a stranger
    To save some poor soul
    Who was already
    Dead
    And gone

    Ben risked his life
And I risked mine for his
And somehow
And for some reason
I feel more human
And more compassion
Than I have felt for a long long time

A Candle Burns Down Low

I tell them I will stay on watch
And they know I will

Bill is the last to leave
A gentle pat on my shoulder
And I can hear him humming
Silent night
As he drifts away
Into the darkness

There is a solitary candle lit
By his bedside
As I settle down
For my vigil

I am exhausted
But not tired
Weary
But wide awake
As I pick up the pocketbook
And hold it gently in my hands

Can these words
Bring comfort
To dying men?

I open the book
The book of John's gospel
And read
About a light shining in the darkness
About a man who defeated
The enemy called death
I read it all
From cover to cover
As the candle burns down low
And Ben's breathing becomes shallower
And shallower

    I read it all

    The light
    Shining
    In the darkness

    And Jesus
    The Light of the World
    Dying
    And
    Rising
    Again

    I read it all

    But do I believe it all?

    I read it all

    But do I believe it at all?

    And as I read
    My eyes
    Become as heavy as lead

And
The book slips from my grasp
The candle dies out
As I feel myself slipping
Into the darkness
Half aware of Ben
And hardly aware
Of a presence
In the room
Not sure if the knife I see
Is in my dream
As my head slumps to my chest

'I knew I'd seen gold'

I am asleep
For a moment
My body slumped
As my eyes flicker open
And in the shadows of night
I see him
I can hear his footsteps

He is coming
And this is no nightmare
But a living hell
He is coming
The man with the knife
In his hand
Is coming

My body is beyond exhausted
My friend hanging like a thread
Between life and death
And there is a man
In the room
A man with a knife
In his hand

The man moves quietly
Silently
Towards Ben

'Good,' he says
'Our two heroes are fast asleep
Or maybe dead'
He laughs as he says it
He is still laughing
As he grabs hold
Of Ben's wrist

'I knew I'd seen gold'
He says

'And I bet there's more where this comes from
A rich lad like you
And where you are going
You are not going to need it
But I am
So I am sure you won't mind'

I never liked Jack
But now I am filled with fury
As I bolt upright
And reach out for his throat

Jack is startled
But he quickly recovers
As he swishes the knife
    As he swishes the sharp blade
    As he swishes the knife
In my face

The Knife and the Watch

I duck
And the blade skims
Through my hair
And from my crouching position
I charge Jack

My headbutt winds him
As he groans
And stumbles backwards
Before he tumbles
And lands with a whack
On the wooden floor

The knife is thrown from his hand
And I scoop it up

'What do you think you are doing?
Robbing a sick soldier!'

Jack rubs his head as he growls and says
'He don't need no gold watch
Not where he's going'

I gaze at Jack
And shake my head
'He's going nowhere'

I tell him
'And if you don't want to be court-martialed
Then you better get out of here'

Jack glares at me
'What about my knife?'

'Happy Christmas Jack
And thanks for the gift'

Jack looks at me but
Says nothing

And leaves
Muttering curses
As he goes

I shake my head
And take a deep breath
What is this world coming to?

I turn round
And sit back down

'Well done soldier'

Ben!

His eyes are open
And he's smiling

'That wasn't Father Christmas, was it?'
He says with a grin

Out Here in France

He should be resting
Not talking
He probably should be dying
Not living
But I'm not complaining
There is something special about this man
Something different
And I need to know what it is

He takes a sip of hot coffee
If you can call it that
But as my nan would say
Beggars can't be choosers
And she was right

'I'm sorry you couldn't save him'
I say

Ben nods
'I couldn't save his life
He was too far gone when I got there
But
I could help save his soul'

Ben looks away
And takes another sip of his coffee

'How? How could you save him? How?'

Ben's face looks solemn
In the glow of the candlelight

'For all of this madness and slaughter
For all of man's inhumanity to man
I believe with all of my heart
That there is a God in Heaven
Who saw the mess of this world
And who sent His Son to save us
Christmas isn't just a fable story
Of shepherds and wise men
But the plan God had for fallen man
The birth of a Saviour
And I have never been more convinced
Of our need for a Saviour
Than out here in France'

Ben looks me in the eyes
    As he says

'Harry, this place may be
As close to Hell as you can imagine
But I also know a God in Heaven
Who can give you peace
Beyond understanding
And a life that is everlasting'

Songs in the Trenches

Christmas morning dawns
With few words spoken
I haven't said much
Since Ben shared his thoughts last night

As much as I had felt heartache
And heartbreak
Beyond what I can bare
And as much as I have despaired
Of life itself
There is something in this story
And something in this pocket Bible
That has stirred something
Deep within me

For the first time in my life
I had thanked God for Christmas
And thanked God for the Christ child

I am still living in Hell
But I am beginning to believe in Heaven

That's when it happens
When the singing starts
When the Germans sing
Like a heavenly choir

And when Bill leads our lads in response
I am not much of a singer
So I didn't join in
Besides I am still looking after Ben
But it is when the singing stops
That Ben speaks

'Do you like football?' he asks

I stare at him
'Used to play all the time'
I say

'I think today will be a great day to play'

The words hang in the silence

'You must be joking!'
    I tell him

Ben smiles

'That would be . . .
That would be a flipping miracle!'

Ben grins and tells me

'I can see that football underneath your bunk . . .
Happy Christmas, Harry'

A Great Day

'How about a game?'
He asks

I listen to the question
And leave it hanging in the air
Like some festive Christmas decoration

'You've got a ball'
He says
A statement
Not a question

I shake my head

'I don't know why I brought it with me'
I confess
'Some kind of keepsake from home
Some kind of touchstone
With my past
With my team
With who I am'

I look at him

'Don't know if that makes any sense'
I say

Ben is smiling like Scrooge who's just woken up
And found out it's Christmas Day
And he hasn't missed it
And now he's ready to enjoy it

'I think today
Being Christmas Day . . .'
Says Ben
Leaving a dramatic pause
'Is a good day to play'

I say nothing
But my hand reaches underneath my bunk
And my hand rolls the ball out

'Go on'
Ben tells me
'Time for a game'
He says

'And don't worry about winning'
He suddenly looks serious
'The game would be the biggest victory'

'See you soon'
I tell him
As I head towards the ladder

A Great Day to Play

The grey dawn matches the greyness of the world
There has been little light for far too long

Winter has felt like a forever season
But today
Right here
Right now
There is something happening that no dark cloud
can deny
That no lingering shadows of night can ever
sweep away

A light

A light
Within

A light
That sparked into life
The moment my heart prayed

My early morning Christmas prayers were so
much more than a nod to God on the birthday of
His Son

It was real

It was personal

It was the hand of a drowning man
Reaching on out

It was the cry of a fallen child
Shouting on out

It was real

And it feels real now as I hold my football
In the palms of my hand

It feels surreal as I walk towards steps that
normally lead into the lions' hungry lair
That normally lead into the soul's agonising
despair

But today
Right here
Right now
These fragile steps

These

Fragile

Steps

Are like a stairway to Heaven

A Battered and Bruised Soul

There was something deeply magical about
Christmas
When I was a child
When war was a word I had never heard
When peace on earth
Was being with family
Being with friends
Simply being with the ones you love
When presents were more about the people than
the gifts they gave you
When the songs that you sang in church
Chimed bells of hope
Rang loud and clear into a bright crisp New Year

When I was a child
When war was a distant word
When peace was more than a frail feather in a
hurricane wind

I'm young
But no longer a child

I'm young
Young in a faith
That has found this battered

And bruised
Lost soul of mine

I am young in seeing the light of day
In seeing the light of the world
Shining in my life
On this Christmas Day

But I'm starting to believe in miracles

Fritz is shaking hands
And offering gifts

Is this peace on earth?

No Longer an Enemy

For a moment
I cannot move

For a moment
I cannot breathe

For a moment
Choirs could be singing

Angelic ones

It feels like that kind of moment

The face of my enemy
Who is no longer a stranger
The face of my enemy
Who is no longer
A danger to me

And I believe

And I am a believer

A believer
In miracles at Christmas

And I believe

And I am a believer

In the miracle of Christmas

And I believe

And I am a believer

In the Christ of Christmas

Especially Now,
Especially Today

I haven't brought my football all the way to the
battlefields of France
Just to give it away
Kick it away
Or watch it be booted into the mud and the mire
Get busted on the rusty barbed wire

It might be Christmas Day
But
It's my ball
My football
And if anyone is going to kick it
The first to play a game with it
Then it's going to be me

A game?

The thought sounds like magi are on their way
Running late
But knowing they're bringing the sweetest and
finest of gifts
Gold
Frankincense

And
Myrrh

Gold
For a king
Frankincense
For a priest
And myrrh
Myrrh for a ...

Myrrh for a ...

... sacrificial death

I don't want to dwell
On death
Not as the light begins to break through
On this miraculous Christmas morning

But I know that Jesus
Is more than a baby
In a manger
And that Jesus was no stranger
To suffering
And the agony
And the anguish
Of a horrifying cross

I am still holding the ball
Not wanting to let it go
When I see him

I see him walking towards me
And before I can see his face
I know
I just know who he is

I kick the ball

I watch it roll
In the mud

Get stuck in the mud

But I know it's right
To give it away

Especially now

Especially today

And especially to the Fritz
Who has walked towards it

Who We All Are

I know before I take a step towards him
Before my feet begin to move
And before I begin to run

Through the wastelands
Through this land that no man should ever know
That no one should ever see

But somehow I know
That I'm seen
That I'm known
That I'm loved
By a Saviour unseen

And I know that my enemy
Is seen too
And not just by me

And I know that I know
Who this enemy is
That is limping
But smiling
Limping
But
Smiling foe

And I know he is only seeing the light
Of this Christmas Day
Because I couldn't face
Taking his life away

I stop running

I'm standing
Before my enemy

The man

The boy

That I walked away from
That I left unharmed
As he extends his arm
And holds out
His hand
To me

I don't shake his hand

I can't

I don't look him in the eyes

I can't

I grab hold of him
Tight

And I hug him
As if he is my long-lost brother

Because

In a way

That's who he is

Because

In a way
That's who we all are

Lost

Until found

Lost

Until rescued

I look up
Look around
See coats on the ground
Coats for goalposts
Just like when we were kids

I smile at Fritz
Who grins back
And says
'Hanz'

'Happy Christmas Hanz
It's time to play football'

Free Lesson Plan for Schools and Churches

The book *Silent Night* offers a unique opportunity for teachers to engage students in meaningful learning experiences. Two freely available lesson plans have been developed by an experienced teacher to complement the book.

Schools

The plans have been written to ensure that they meet the needs of upper KS2 and lower KS3 students. These lesson plans have been crafted with the National Curriculum and SACRE guidelines in mind, guaranteeing a high-quality educational experience, thereby saving teachers valuable planning time. An online resources area is also included as well as ideas for subsequent lessons, offering opportunities for progression in learning.

Churches

Churches may choose to read *Silent Night* with older children's groups, youth groups or in home groups. The lesson plans can be used as starting points for discussion around the importance of sharing testimonies and for boldness in sharing the good new of Jesus with those around us. In these contexts, which vary in duration and age groups, it may be useful to divide the lessons into shorter segments and to encourage reading of the book between group sessions. These resources would be ideal for using around Remembrance Sunday or during the season of Advent.

About the Lessons
One of the lesson plans takes a cross-curricular approach, focusing on History and RE. This plan delves into the true events of the Christmas Truce, which is the central theme of the book. By exploring this historical event, students will gain a deeper understanding of the context and significance of the story. This approach will help students develop their critical thinking skills and encourages a growing empathy for people whose lives are challenged and changed by war.

The other is an English lesson plan and focuses on the genre of Free Verse – the form in which *Silent Night* is written. Students are encouraged to break free from the constraints of traditional poetic forms, embracing instead the freedom to express themselves through unstructured and emotive language. This mode of creative writing allows students to tap into their inner worlds, exploring themes and ideas that are unique to their individual experiences. By immersing themselves in this style through the reading of the book, students will be able to produce beautiful written pieces for displays and for presentation.

History and RE Lesson Plan
Download now!

www.malcolmdown.co.uk/lesson-plan/history

Silent Night Lesson Plan
Download now!

www.malcolmdown.co.uk/lesson-plan/silent-night

About the Author

Tony Bower is the CEO of York Schools and Youth Trust (YoYo) who work with schools and churches to bring the Christian faith alive. He is also a freelance writer, poet and speaker. He is married to Claire, and they have one son, Joseph, who is married to Taryana.

Tony and Claire also have a fun, bouncy dog called Monty.

Printed in Dunstable, United Kingdom

72140497R00050

Christmas Eve, 1914.

In the war-torn trenches, far from home, one young soldier
faces an impossible choice when fear is anything but silent.

When a cry for help echoes across No Man's Land, Harry must
decide what sort of man he wants to be – loyal, compassionate
or both.

And yet, even in the darkness of war, a glimmer of light begins
to shine – through singing soldiers, a football, and coats being
used as goalposts.

Emotionally rich and historically inspired, this free verse
narrative brings hope and light to the darkest of times as the
mysterious Christmas spirit pierces through.

Tony Bower is the EO of York Schools and Youth Trust (YoYo)
who work with schools and churches to bring the Christian
faith alive. He is also a freelance writer, poet and speaker. He is
married to Claire, and they have one son, Joseph, who is
married to Taryana.

md
PUBLISHING
www.malcolmdown.co.uk

ISBN 978-1-917455-49-7

9 781917 455497 >